Jemma's Big Leap

by Kathryn England
illustrated by Bobbie Moynihan

Scholastic Canada Ltd.

Characters

Jemma

Mr. Rizzoli

Contents

Chapter 1
A New Footpath   4

Chapter 2
Jemma's Print   10

Chapter 3
A Cement Suit   20

Chapter 4
Hot Days   26

Chapter 1

A New Footpath

Jemma lived on a street with no sidewalks. In fact, there was grass all the way to the store.

Jemma liked the feel of cool grass between her toes. If she had to cross a prickly weed patch, she'd tiptoe through it or jump right over it.

One day, Jemma was walking to the store to buy a drink. She turned a corner and saw that the grass was gone.

Orange and white plastic strips were tied between the posts. A sign said WET CEMENT.

Jemma could almost hear the wet cement calling her. In an oozy sort of voice it said, "Hello there, feet. Want to leave your prints here? Go on. I dare you."

She chewed her bottom lip and looked up and down the street. A car drove up and over the hill. There was no one else around.

Jemma's Print

Very slowly, she slid her big toe over the bottom strip and poked it into the wet cement. Her toe made a circle shape.

She crawled between the plastic strips.

Jemma could hear a truck roaring up the hill. Once it got to the top, the driver would see her.

Jemma would have to hurry. She jumped.

It was a mistake. The wet cement was slippery. Jemma's arms spun like windmills.

Jemma bellyflopped onto the cement.

The cement tasted awful. It was horrible and gritty.

Little shivers ran up and down Jemma's spine as cement crunched between her teeth.

Bits of cement stuck to Jemma's hair and dangled in front of her eyes.

"Are you all right?" a man asked.

The truck driver was leaning out of the window. It was Mr. Rizzoli, Jemma's neighbour.

"Let me give you a hand," he said.

Mr. Rizzoli jumped out of his truck with a big grin on his face.

His eyes crinkled, and he cleared his throat. "Lucky for you I had to come back. I left my trowel behind."

"Fell through, did you?" Mr. Rizzoli asked in a squeaky voice.

"Sort of," Jemma mumbled.

"If you weren't looking, it would be easy to trip." Mr. Rizzoli turned his head away to hide his laughter.

A Cement Suit

Jemma learned a couple of things that day. She learned that wet cement makes clothes really heavy.

The other thing she learned was that wet cement dries fast. It was like wearing a suit of armour.

The cement on Jemma's face, arms and legs dried and began to crack.

"I'll give you a lift home," Mr. Rizzoli said.

He threw his trowel into the truck and climbed into the driver's seat.

At her house, Jemma thanked him. She climbed down from the truck.

"Got to get back to work," Mr. Rizzoli called.

He gave a cheery wave and drove off. You could hear him laughing all the way down the street.

Hot Days

The new cement footpath was dry the next day.

But Jemma never walks on it.

If she feels like a drink or an ice cream she always walks on the grass.

It's longer, but she doesn't mind. She likes to walk barefoot on the cool grass.

Jemma doesn't like to walk along the new sidewalk. It's too hot. But there is also another reason!

Glossary

armour
hard clothing worn to protect the body

bellyflopped
fell flat on one's tummy

cement
liquid rock that becomes hard when it dries

crinkled
wrinkled with laughter

dare
to challenge someone to do something

gritty
sandy, stony

oozy
slimy

prickly
thorny, sharp

prints
footprints

trowel
a tool used to spread cement

Kathryn England

I live on a street with no sidewalks. Some streets in my area have concrete sidewalks. These are the main things I like and don't like about sidewalks.

Grass	Nice green colour if watered often	✓
	Prickly if not watered often!	✗
Sidewalks	Good for rollerblading	✓
	Bad for toe stubbing!	✗

Bobbie Moynihan